LEOLA
AND THE
HONEYBEARS

An African-American Retelling of
GOLDILOCKS AND THE THREE BEARS

Melodye Benson Rosales

SCHOLASTIC INC.   Cartwheel BOOKS®

New York   Toronto   London   Auckland   Sydney
Mexico City   New Delhi   Hong Kong

"Look, Grandmama! Look!" Leola sang out as she struggled to pull the biggest, wettest bedsheet from the laundry basket.

Monday was always wash day, and much to her grandmother's surprise, Leola had decided to help hang out the sheets.

"Listen, child! Just put that sheet down before you get it all full of dirt!" fussed Leola's grandmother.

Leola sighed. "But I just wanted to help."

"I know, sugar pie, but I don't need any help right now," Grandmama replied. "You go on and play now. But don't go straying off anywhere. And don't go talking to any strangers!" Then she went back to her wash.

When she looked up again, Leola was merrily dancing away, headed for the nearby meadow.

"YOU HEAR ME, LEOLA?" Grandmama shouted after her. "Mind me, and don't go straying off!"

Leola did hear her grandmother, but she paid her no mind. She didn't even answer her.

Leola and her grandmother lived in a small, cozy cottage not far from the Pine Hollow Woods. When Leola got her way, she could be as sweet as brown sugar. But when she didn't, she could be as stubborn as Grandmama's old mule.

Today Leola could find nothing fun to do. "I'm bored," she complained. "And I don't care what my Grandmama says. I'm going to do what I want to."

Suddenly, Leola caught sight of some milkweed seeds blowing in the breeze across the meadow. "*O-o-o-w-e-e!*" she squealed as she watched the silky pods float farther and farther from the cottage. Off she ran, chasing after them.

After running for a while, Leola finally looked back. Nothing looked familiar. But Leola didn't care. She was having too much fun, following the cotton-like balls....

right into the Pine Hollow Woods!

Before she knew it, Leola was surrounded by prickly bushes and towering pine trees. The sunlight had all but disappeared. She turned around full circle, but she couldn't tell which way was home.

"Oh, no!" cried Leola as she stared into the darkness. "I must be lost."

Now way down deep in the Pine Hollow Woods stood a charming little inn. It was owned by a family known as the Honeybears. Papa Honeybear was a GREAT, BIG bear. Mama Honeybear was a MIDDLE-SIZED bear. Lil' Honey was LITTLE, just like his name.

Woodland folks from far and near came to visit the Honeybears' inn. They dined on delicious daily delights like dandelion stew, double-dipped daffodil custard, and sweet daisy-dough cakes. Cheerful chatter and hearty laughter always filled the inn.

Come evening time, Papa Honeybear sat in his GREAT, BIG oak chair and gobbled his GREAT, BIG toasted walnuts. Mama Honeybear sat in her MIDDLE-SIZED easy chair and munched her MIDDLE-SIZED roasted chestnuts. And Lil' Honey sat in his LITTLE wooden chair and nibbled his LITTLE chocolate-covered pinenuts.

On this particular morning, after Mama Honeybear had served the last of her boysenberry grits to Mister Hare and his grandbaby, Bunnie, she decided to make some special treats for her own family. She baked a GREAT, BIG plum pie for Papa Honeybear and a MIDDLE-SIZED rose petal cobbler for herself, and a LITTLE huckleberry tart for Lil' Honey.

When Papa Honeybear and Lil' Honey had finished their morning chores, they were as hungry as, well…bears.

"Oh, darlings," chuckled Mama Honeybear, "those pies just came out of the stove. They're much too hot now. Why don't we head over to Parson's Pond and catch a mess of catfish? By the time we get back, I'm sure the pies will be cool enough to eat."

Meanwhile, poor Leola was still wandering around the deepest, darkest part of the Pine Hollow Woods. "I promise always to listen to my Grandmama, no matter how much I want to do what I want to," Leola said, "just please let me find my way back home."

Weary and confused, Leola plopped down on a damp patch of ground. Suddenly the cool forest air filled with a warm, sweet smell.

"That must be my Grandmama's cracklin' biscuits baking," said Leola. "Now I know I can find my way...."

But before Leola could finish, Ol' Mister Weasel came slowly slinking by.

"Howdy, sweet Lil' Missy," he said in his oily voice. Ol' Mister Weasel gave a sly smirk as he hungrily licked his lips.

Leola quickly hopped to her feet at the sight of the stranger.

Ol' Mister Weasel laughed out loud. "Now, now child, I don't mean to scare you none." He slithered around, this way and that way.... "I'm jus' wantin' to *eat you whole!*"

With that, Leola took off running as fast as her feet could carry her, following the sweet smell that still filled the woods. Soon she came to a large clearing. As Leola wiped the sweat from her brow, she saw a little house in the distance.

"That must be a stranger's house," Leola thought to herself as she looked back over her shoulder for Ol' Mister Weasel. "I know my Grandmama told me about strangers. But I can't go back 'cause Ol' Mister Weasel will eat me for sure!" So Leola headed straight for the Honeybears' inn.

She knocked on the heavy wooden door, but no one answered. The door was open just a little, so she poked her head in.

"Hello!" Leola hollered. "Excuse me, please. Are you folks in?" Still no one answered.

"I know my Grandmama said, 'Never go inside folks' houses until first being politely asked,' but I don't think she'd mind *this time*." And she quietly crept inside.

The first thing to catch Leola's eye were the tasty-looking treats sitting out on the kitchen counter.

"*O-o-o-w-e-e!*" Leola squealed. "I'm so hungry. I know my Grandmama said, 'Never help yourself in folks' kitchens until first being politely asked,' but I don't think she'd mind *this time.*"

So Leola stuck her small finger into Papa Honeybear's GREAT, BIG plum pie and tasted it. "*O-o-o-h, no!*" Leola cried as she puckered her lips. It was much too sour.

Then she took a taste from Mama Honeybear's MIDDLE-SIZED rose petal cobbler. "*O-o-o-h, no!*" It was much too sweet. Finally, she tasted Lil' Honey's LITTLE huckleberry tart and it was absolutely delicious! Leola gobbled it down, right then and there.

"Oh, I'm *so* tired," Leola said as she let out a big yawn.

"I know my Grandmama said, '*Never* sit down in folks' houses until first being politely asked,' but I don't think she'd mind *this time*."

Leola was beginning to feel right at home. First, she sat in Papa Honeybear's GREAT, BIG chair. But it was much too hard. And so were his toasted walnuts.

Then she sat in Mama Honeybear's MIDDLE-SIZED chair. But it was much too soft. And so were her roasted chestnuts.

Finally, Leola sat in Lil' Honey's LITTLE wooden chair. It felt like it was made just for her, and she loved his chocolate-covered pinenuts! She ate every one, "Yummy, yum, yum!"

Before long, Leola had stuffed herself so full of huckleberry tart and chocolate-covered pine nuts that the buttons on her dress began to pull and her tummy began to ache....

And, then, K$_A$B$_O^{O}_M$!

Lil' Honey's LITTLE wooden chair broke all to pieces!

"Oh, my," Leola moaned. "I know my Grandmama said, 'Never make yourself *too* comfortable in folks' houses until first being politely asked,' but I don't think she'd mind *this time*."

Leola dragged herself up from the floor to look for a place to lie down.

At the top of the stairs Leola found the Honeybear's bedroom with three neatly made beds all in a row.

First, she lay down on Papa Honeybear's GREAT, BIG bed. But it was much too hard.

Then, she lay down on Mama Honeybear's MIDDLE-SIZED bed, but it was much too soft.

Finally, she lay down on Lil' Honey's LITTLE bed. And it was just right! Without another yawn, Leola fell fast asleep.

By this time, the Honeybears were on their way home, laughing and singing their favorite fishing song:

Many fish are in the brook, Papa caught 'em with a hook.
Mama fried 'em in a pan, Baby eat 'em like a man!

When Papa Honeybear swung open the door, the Honeybears could not believe their eyes. Their cozy little inn looked like a strong gust of wind had just whipped through it. Everything was upside down and inside out!

"LOOK!" growled Papa Honeybear in his GREAT, BIG bear voice. "Somebody's been eating my plum pie."

"And look!" cried Mama Honeybear in her MIDDLE-SIZED bear voice. "Somebody's been eating my rose petal cobbler!"

"And look!" squealed Lil' Honey in his LITTLE bear voice. "Somebody ate *every* bit of my huckleberry tart!"

"LOOK!" Papa Honeybear growled in his GREAT, BIG bear voice. "Somebody's been sitting in my chair, eating my walnuts."

"And somebody's been sitting in my chair," cried Mama Honeybear in her MIDDLE-SIZED voice. "And they left chestnuts all over it."

"And somebody helped themselves to *all* my chocolate-covered pinenuts and broke my chair *all* to pieces!" squealed Lil' Honey in his LITTLE voice as his LITTLE brown eyes welled up with tears.

"Sh-h-h!" Mama Honeybear whispered. "What's that strange sound?"

With Papa Honeybear leading the way, they all tiptoed up the stairs. They crept past Papa Honeybear's GREAT, BIG bed and around Mama Honeybear's MIDDLE-SIZED bed, until they reached Lil' Honey's LITTLE bed, and they gasped at what they saw.

"Look!" squealed Lil' Honey. "A stranger!"

Startled, Leola woke up and saw three angry-looking bears leaning over her!

"*Oh, please, don't eat me!*" Leola cried.

"We're not going to eat you," Mama Honeybear said sternly. "But didn't your folks teach you any manners?"

"Yes, m-m-ma'am," Leola stammered. "My Grandmama always told me, '*Never* to go into folks' houses…and *never* help yourself in folks' kitchens…and never, *ever* sit down and make yourself too comfortable until first being politely asked,' but I couldn't find my way back home and Ol' Mister Weasel tried to eat me and I was so scared and hungry I didn't think anyone would mind, *just this time*."

As the tears flowed down Leola's face, Mama Honeybear saw that she was only a youngster, no different than her own Lil' Honey. Soon, all was forgiven.

Mama Honeybear took her best straw basket, stuffed it full of scrumptious treats, and covered it with one of her prettiest lace doilies.

As she handed the basket to Leola, Mama Honeybear called to Miss Blackbird, who was hovering overhead. "Miss Blackbird, would you mind guiding this child back home? We don't want her getting lost again."

"Why surely, Mama Honey," Miss Blackbird replied. "But we need to get going, child. It'll be dark soon."

Mama Honeybear gave Leola a tender good-bye bear hug. "You were lucky this time, Leola," she said. "But you might not be the next. Your Grandmama told you right. She must love you very much."

Leola had taken only a few steps down the path when she turned to wave at her new friends. Mama Honeybear pulled Lil' Honey extra close and Papa Honeybear put his arm around her as they all waved good-bye.

As Leola neared the open meadow, she smelled fresh-washed laundry flapping in the breeze. With home in sight, she heard her Grandmama calling—and this time, Leola did answer back!

From that day on—even when she wanted to do what she wanted to—Leola always listened to her Grandmama. (Well...most of the time.) And she never strayed too far from home again.

*This book is dedicated to all the grandmothers who
have loved and cared for their grandchildren.*

＞—⬦—◇—⬦—＜

My great-grandmother, Ellen Weathersby, was born into slavery in a rural community
in Lawrence County, Mississippi. She married the "Mulatto" son of the plantation's
owner, my great-grandfather Sanco Benson. Together, Ellen and Sanco had 11 children.
They raised them with an abundance of patience and guidance.

During this time, after slavery had been abolished, Sanco farmed the
land...his land. Ellen made their house into a home. When their grandchildren
were born, Ellen tenderly cared for them as well. It was a large family
and her 23 grandchildren filled her days with joy and happiness.

Ellen, an enormous woman in size and stature, as well as love
and affection, was known throughout the county for raising another
thing of beauty—colorful flower gardens. Her son, my maternal
grandfather, Papa Benson, would often tell me he thought my great-
grandmother's spirit lived on in me by way of my artistic expression
and appreciation of colors. I know it does.

This story is a reflection of memories. Memories of growing up with old-fashioned
values in a family filled to the brim with love and understanding. Memories that are
part of many families. Memories that are part of "my" family, the Bensons.

WITH SPECIAL THANKS TO:

Bernette Ford, my editor, whose timeless ideas are entrusted to me to breathe life into them;
Edie Weinberg, my art director, who encourages my visions with mega-doses of patience;
Kimberly Weinberger, associate editor, who kept all the pieces glued, dotted the "i's" and crossed the "t's";
Debbie Cobb, art traffic manager, for making sure my artwork was carefully handled (and dry!);
Kaye Benson, my sister, who will always be the mentor of my words;
Dino Malcolm, my creative buddy, who believed in "Leola" from the start;
Professor William Berry, UIUC, for his critical ear and the ability to listen;
Professor Violet J. Harris, UIUC, for her professional ear and friendship;
Houston Bethel Jr., who helped to fill my head with memories and my heart with a sense of family;
Chris, my anchor, and my *Mom*—it all started with you.

＞—⬦—◇—⬦—＜

Copyright © 1999 by Melodye Benson Rosales.
All rights reserved. Published by Scholastic Inc.
SCHOLASTIC, CARTWHEEL BOOKS and the CARTWHEEL BOOKS
logo are trademarks and/or registered trademarks of Scholastic Inc.

Library of Congress Cataloging-in-Publication Data

Rosales, Melodye Benson.
    Leola and the honeybears / written and illustrated by Melodye Benson Rosales.
        p.   cm.
    "Cartwheel books."
    Summary: An African-American version of Goldilocks and the three bears.
    ISBN 0-590-38358-2
    [1. Folklore.]   I. Title.
    PZ8.1.R6815Le   1998
    398.22—dc21   97-31871
                                                                      CIP
                                                                       AC

10 9 8 7 6 5 4 3 2 1   9/9 0/0 01 02 03 04
                Printed in Mexico   49
                First printing, October 1999